MORE
DANIEL TIGER
5-Minute Stories

Simon Spotlight

New York   London   Toronto   Sydney   New Delhi

SIMON SPOTLIGHT

An imprint of Simon & Schuster Children's Publishing Division

1230 Avenue of the Americas, New York, New York 10020

This Simon Spotlight edition August 2020

For information about special discounts for bulk purchases, please contact Simon & Schuster Special Sales at 1-866-506-1949 or business@simonandschuster.com.

Manufactured in China 0620 WGL

10 9 8 7 6 5 4 3 2 1

ISBN 978-1-5344-7114-6

ISBN 978-1-5344-7115-3 (eBook)

These titles were previously published individually by Simon Spotlight with slightly different text and art.

Contents

Daniel's First Babysitter 4

Daniel Has an Allergy 20

Daniel's Potty Time 40

Daniel Learns to Ride a Bike 52

Mama Travels for Work 68

No Red Sweater for Daniel 82

Daniel Chooses to Be Kind 100

Daniel Plays in the Snow 122

Calm at the Restaurant 134

Munch Your Lunch! 148

Big Enough to Help 162

Daniel Tiger's Day and Night 180

Daniel's First Babysitter

It was a beautiful day in the neighborhood, and Daniel was playing jungle with Tigey before bed.

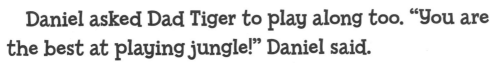

Daniel asked Dad Tiger to play along too. "You are the best at playing jungle!" Daniel said.

But Dad couldn't play. "Sorry, my fuzzy guy," Dad said. "Remember, Mom and I are going out. Look who's here to take care of you!"

"Prince Tuesday! I'm getting a babysitter tonight!" Daniel said with excitement.

Prince Tuesday said, "I will take rrroyally good care of you until your parents come back home."

Dad said, "And when we get back home and you're asleep, we'll give you a kiss."

8

Daniel smiled, and he sang, *"Grown-ups come back."*

After Mom and Dad left, Daniel asked, "But now who's going to play jungle with me?"

"Your babysitter can!" said Prince Tuesday. "Watch out for that snake!" He jumped into the cave, and Daniel followed.

Daniel's babysitter was fun to play jungle with, just like Dad Tiger.

It was almost Daniel's bedtime. Prince Tuesday said, "Let's go through the jungle to get to your room!"

Mom Tiger and Dad Tiger usually help Daniel get ready for bed. Daniel asked, "Who will help me pick out my pajamas?"

"Your babysitter can!" said Prince Tuesday. Daniel's babysitter helped pick out his favorite Trolley pajamas, just like Mom and Dad.

15

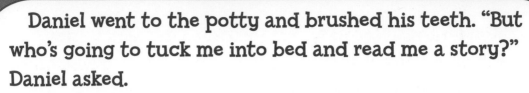

Daniel went to the potty and brushed his teeth. "But who's going to tuck me into bed and read me a story?" Daniel asked.

"Your babysitter can!" said Prince Tuesday.

Daniel was all ready for bed, except . . . he couldn't find Tigey! "Mom and Dad always know where Tigey is," said Daniel. "Now who will help me find Tigey?"

"Your babysitter can!" said Prince Tuesday. They looked all around the house.

"Do you see Tigey?" asked Daniel. He was worried.

They looked some more and soon found Tigey! Daniel got back into bed.

Mom and Dad came home, just like they said they would. They quietly sang, "*Grown-ups come back.♩♪* Goodnight, Daniel. Goodnight, Tigey. Ugga Mugga!"

Daniel Has an Allergy

Daniel had never eaten a peach before.
"Do you want to try a peach?" asked Dad.
"Sure," said Daniel.
Daniel took a bite. It was deeeeee-licious!

But then Daniel started to feel itchy. His face felt itchy and his legs felt itchy.

Mom noticed that Daniel had some red bumps on his face. "Does anything else bother you?" asked Mom. "My tummy kind of hurts," said Daniel.

"I think we should go to Dr. Anna's office so she can check you out," said Dad.

Dad and Daniel boarded Trolley to go to Dr. Anna's office. "Am I going to be okay?" Daniel asked.

"You're going to be okay because Dr. Anna will take care of you," said Dad. "She will figure out why you are itchy and why your tummy hurts."

Daniel felt a little better. Then Dad sang, "We take care of each other." ♪ ♫

Daniel and Dad arrived at Dr. Anna's office.
"What did you eat today?" Dr. Anna asked Daniel.
"I had blueberries and oatmeal for breakfast, and then I tried peaches for the first time," said Daniel.
"Ah!" said Dr. Anna. "You could be allergic to peaches."

"Allergic?" Daniel asked.

"That means your body doesn't like peaches," Dr. Anna explained. "They give you these itchy bumps—or hives—on your face and legs, and a tummy ache when you eat them."

27

Dr. Anna gave Daniel some medicine that would make him feel better.

"*We take care of each other,*" Dr. Anna sang. She was happy to help.

"But I also need you to take care of yourself," Dr. Anna said.

She gave Daniel three rules to follow.

Rule 1: Don't eat the food that you're allergic to.

Rule 2: If you don't feel well, tell a grown-up.

Rule 3: Ask before you eat something new to make sure you are not allergic.

Dad and Daniel left Dr. Anna's office. Daniel felt better.

"So if someone gives me peaches, I just say 'no, thank you'?" Daniel asked.

"Right," said Dad. "You can say 'yes, thank you' to bananas, blueberries, and strawberries."

Daniel liked all those foods!

That gave him an idea.

Do you want to make believe with Daniel?

Daniel imagined he was in a video game. He sang a song!

*Allergies! Allergies!
Pineapple, pizza, watermelon
pieces, Daniel Tiger needs to
avoid the peaches.
Tomatoes, beets?
My favorite treats!
Bananas and
toast? I can
eat both!*

*Allergies! Allergies!
Veggie stew? Don't
mind if I do! How
about a slice of
peach? No, that's
not for me. He
doesn't eat them so
he won't feel sick.
Allergies! Allergies!*

At home Daniel shared everything he learned with Mom.

But then he remembered. He was supposed to make a peach pie to bring to school!

"Oh no." Daniel sighed. "Now we can't make peach pie."

"Let's figure out something new we can bake together," said Mom.

Daniel looked around the kitchen. He saw the peaches, but he couldn't have them.

"Do you see a fruit you can have?" asked Mom.

There were lots of fruits Daniel could have. He could have oranges and apples and bananas!

"How about we make banana bread muffins?" Daniel asked.

"Good idea," said Mom. "Let's bake!"

When the muffins were ready, Daniel was very excited to eat one.

"Mmm," Daniel said. "May I try some jam on my muffin?"

But Daniel had never tried jam before. Thanks to his new rules, he knew what to do. He had to ask before trying something new.

"Are there peaches in this?" Daniel asked.
"This jam has no peaches," Mom told him.
Daniel put some jam on his banana muffin. It was deeeeee-licious!

I'm allergic to peaches. But my mom and dad and Dr. Anna took care of me, because we take care of each other. Are you allergic to any foods?
Ugga Mugga!

Daniel's Potty Time

"Hi, neighbor!" said Daniel Tiger. "We're meeting Katerina at the market today. We're going to pick up toppings and make veggie pizza!"

"You should try to go potty before you leave the house," said Mom Tiger.

"I don't have to go potty," replied Daniel. He just wanted to go meet Katerina.

"Okay," said Mom. "But remember, there's no potty on Trolley!"

41

Mom and Daniel buckled up on Trolley. They sang, "We're going to get some vegetables to make a special lunch. Won't you ride along with me?" Then Daniel stopped singing. He started wiggling in his seat.

Daniel realized that he needed to go potty. But there was no potty on Trolley!

"We'll have to stop, turn around, and go back home," said Mom.

"But Katerina is waiting for us at the market." Daniel was worried. "What if she leaves?"

"The most important thing right now is to listen to your body," said Mom. Then she sang, *"Do you have to go potty? Maybe yes. Maybe no. Why don't you sit and try to go?"*

"Okay, I will do that!" said Daniel.

Once they got home, Daniel went to the potty. He wasn't sure if he was done yet, so he sang, *"Do you have to go potty? Maybe yes. Maybe no. Why don't you sit and try to go?"* Daniel sat and waited some more.

Daniel wiped, flushed, and washed his hands. Then he was on his way! "Now we can head to the market," said Mom.

"But, Mom," said Daniel, "*you* didn't go to the potty! *Do you have to go potty? Maybe yes. Maybe no. Why don't you sit and try to go* . . . because there's no potty on ♪ Trolley!"

Mom laughed. Daniel was right. She went to the potty too. Then they were ready to go to the market again.

When they got to the neighborhood market, Daniel couldn't find Katerina. "Maybe she went home," Daniel said sadly.

Katerina was at the treehouse! "Hi, Katerina!" Daniel said. "Can you still come over for lunch?"

"Yes, meow meow!" Katerina replied. "Veggie pizza is so yummy-in-my-tummy!"

Once they arrived at Daniel's house, Daniel and Katerina ran into the kitchen to wash their hands. Mom Tiger rolled out the dough and spread the tomato sauce. Daniel sprinkled cheese and broccoli on top. Katerina added her favorite bell peppers.

Daniel wanted to keep cooking, but his tummy started to hurt.

"When your tummy hurts, that might mean you need to go poop," Mom said. *"Do you have to go potty? Maybe yes. Maybe no. Why don't you sit and try to go?"*

Daniel waited on the potty. He did have to poop! Then he wiped, flushed, and washed his hands. He was ready to cook again!

The veggie pizza turned out deeelicious!
"Next time before you leave the house, you can try
going to the potty too," said Daniel. "Ugga Mugga!"

Daniel Learns to Ride a Bike

It was a beautiful day in the Neighborhood of Make-Believe. Suddenly Daniel heard a sound. It sounded like ringing! Daniel looked around to see where the sound was coming from.

Daniel walked through his yard, past his playhouse, until he found . . .

. . . Dad Tiger standing next to a shiny red bike, ringing the bell. *Ring! Ring!*

"Dad!" said Daniel. "Why do you have a bike?"

"This was my bike when I was a little tiger," Dad told Daniel. "But now I'm giving it to you!"

Daniel gave Dad a big hug. "Thank you, Dad. Can I ride it now?"

"You sure can," said Dad. "Let's put your helmet on first, and then we can go."

"Yay!" said Daniel happily.

Dad helped Daniel get on the bike, and he started to pedal.

"Here I go! *Vroom! Vroom!*" said Daniel, giggling.

Daniel wiggled and wobbled. He wobbled and he wiggled.

"Riding this bike is hard!" he said.

"Riding a bike *is* hard," said Dad. "But keep working at it! Just *grr-grr-grr out loud. Keep on trying and you'll feel proud!*" ♪ ♫

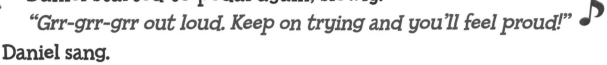

Daniel started to pedal again, slowly.

"Grr-grr-grr out loud. Keep on trying and you'll feel proud!"
Daniel sang.

Daniel wiggled and he wobbled. He wobbled and he wiggled.
And then slowly . . . he started to move forward!

"I'm doing it!" shouted Daniel proudly. "I'm riding my bike!"

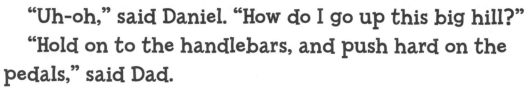

"Uh-oh," said Daniel. "How do I go up this big hill?"

"Hold on to the handlebars, and push hard on the pedals," said Dad.

Daniel held on to the handlebars and pushed hard on the pedals, but he still couldn't make it up the hill!

"Riding up a hill is hard," said Dad, "but I know you can do it. Remember, *grr-grr-grr out loud. Keep on trying and you'll feel proud!*"

Daniel kept on trying. *"Grr-grr-grr,"* he said out loud. Then he pushed and he pedaled up, and up, and up until finally . . .

"I made it to the top of the hill!" said Daniel.

"How do you feel?" asked Dad.

"Proud," said Daniel with a big smile. "And look, there's the park!" He giggled as he continued to pedal.

At the park Daniel saw his friends Prince Wednesday and Chrissie. Prince Wednesday's brother, Prince Tuesday, was there too!

"Royally great bike!" said Prince Wednesday.

"It looks really fast," said Chrissie.

"Thanks," said Daniel. "I like the bell. *Ring! Ring!*"

Daniel, Chrissie, and Prince Wednesday decided to play on the rings.

"I want to swing all the way across," said Prince Wednesday.

"You can do it!" cheered Chrissie.

But when Prince Wednesday tried, he couldn't make it across the rings. Prince Wednesday was upset.

"This is hard," he said sadly.

"You can do it, Prince Wednesday," said Daniel. ♪ ♫
"Grr-grr-grr out loud. Keep on trying and you'll feel proud!"
"Okay, I'll keep trying," said Prince Wednesday.

Prince Wednesday reached for the first ring, and then the second ring, and then the third ring.

"Grr-grr-grr out loud. Keep on trying and you'll feel proud!" Prince Wednesday sang as he reached for each ring. At last Prince Wednesday made it all the way across the rings!

"I did it!" shouted Prince Wednesday. "I feel so proud."

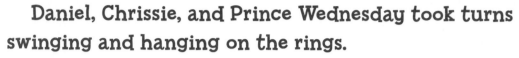

Daniel, Chrissie, and Prince Wednesday took turns swinging and hanging on the rings.

Chrissie could hang on the rings for eight whole seconds without letting go!

"Chrissie is really strong," said Prince Wednesday.

"Riding a bike is hard to do!" said Daniel. "But I *grr*-ed and *grr*-ed and kept trying. And I'm proud that I did it. What are you trying to learn? Ugga Mugga!"

67

Mama Travels for Work

It was a beautiful day in the neighborhood, and Daniel was playing at his neighbor Jodi's house.

"Dr. Plat, why are you putting your dentist clothes in that bag?" asked Daniel.

Dr. Plat explained that she was going on a trip to help some other children clean their teeth.

"She's going away for three whole days," said Jodi.

"Wow," said Daniel. "Three whole days!"

Jodi hugged her mama. "I'm going to miss you so much!"

"I'm going to miss you, too," said Dr. Plat. "But remember that Nana will be here to take care of you, and you will have your love you loops."

"My love you loops!" said Jodi. Then she sang,

 "Love you, love you, love you loops!
Open a loop every day Mama's away.
Love you, love you, love you loops!"

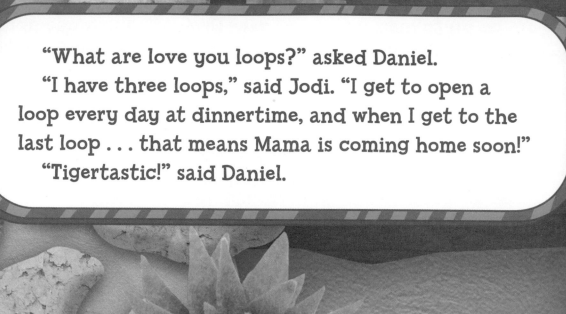

"What are love you loops?" asked Daniel.

"I have three loops," said Jodi. "I get to open a loop every day at dinnertime, and when I get to the last loop . . . that means Mama is coming home soon!"

"Tigertastic!" said Daniel.

It was time for Dr. Plat to leave, so she gave a big hug to Jodi and her brothers, Teddy and Leo.

Jodi didn't want her mama to leave, but Daniel told Jodi what Mom Tiger always told him when she went to work:

 *"Grown-ups come back!"*

Daniel's mom would come back, and Jodi's mama would come back too.

After Dr. Plat left, Jodi hung her love you loops and sang,

"Love you, love you, love you loops!
Open a loop every day Mama's away.
Love you, love you, love you loops!"

Then it was time to play. Daniel and Jodi pretended to be airplanes.

"Look!" said Jodi. "I'm flying to work! Zoom! Zoom! But I'll come back!"

As Daniel and Jodi played, Daniel imagined what it would be like if all his friends went to work just like the grown-ups!

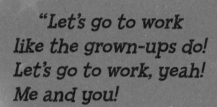

"Let's go to work like the grown-ups do! Let's go to work, yeah! Me and you!

We're doing something we love to do. Working hard like the grown-ups do.

Let's go to work like the grown-ups do!

Work real hard, yeah! Me and you!"

Each day her mama was away, Jodi opened a love you loop and found a surprise from her mama!

The first day, when Jodi opened the first loop, there was a drawing of the cozi-cozi pillow on Jodi's bed. When Jodi went to her bedroom and looked under her pillow, she found sparkly stickers from Mama!

The second day, the love you loop had a picture of the mailbox, and Jodi received a postcard from Mama!

On the third day, there was just one love you loop left. Jodi opened it and saw that it had a picture of a door on it.

"A door? What door?" wondered Daniel.

"Maybe it's *our* door!" said Jodi.

Nana opened the door to Jodi's house, and they saw . . .

. . . Mama! Dr. Plat came back from her trip just like she said she would. Jodi and her brothers were so happy that their mama was home, and their mama was so happy to see them again and hear all about what they had done while she was away!

It wasn't easy for Jodi and her brothers when their mama went away, but now they know:

 "Grown-ups come back!"

Ugga Mugga!

No Red Sweater for Daniel

"It's time to get dressed, Daniel," said Mom Tiger. "We have to go pick up a package at the post office!"

"Okay!" said Daniel.

Daniel went to his room to put on his favorite red sweater. But when he opened his drawer, his red sweater wasn't there! Where was it?

Daniel looked high.

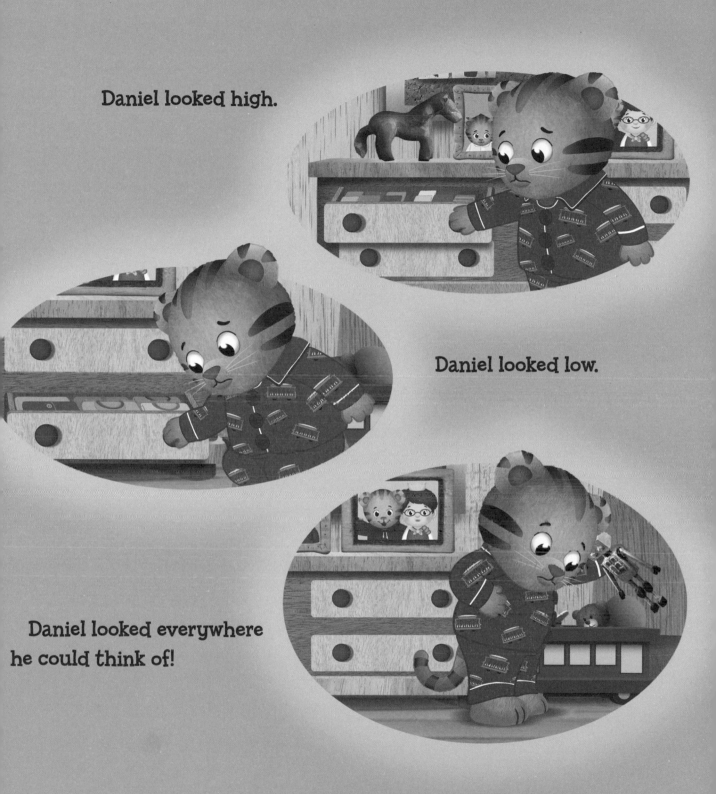

Daniel looked low.

Daniel looked everywhere
he could think of!

But Daniel's red sweater was . . . gone!

"My red sweater is gone!" Daniel said to his mom.

"It isn't gone," said Mom Tiger. "It was dirty, so it's in the wash."

"But I want to wear my red sweater. It's my favorite," said Daniel. Daniel was upset!

"Why don't you wear a different sweater?" asked Mom. "I always wear my red sweater," said Daniel. "If I don't wear it, then I won't be me."

"Yes, you will," said Mom.

 "You can change your hair, or what you wear, but no matter what you do, you're still you."

85

"Okay," said Daniel. "I'll try wearing a different sweater today. I'll wear my blue sweater."

Daniel put on his blue sweater and looked at himself in the mirror. "Wow," he said. "I look different."

"You do look a little different, but you're still Daniel on the inside," said Mom Tiger.

Daniel smiled.

"Come on," said Mom Tiger. "Let's go to the post office."

"Trolley! Please take us to the post office!" said Daniel.
"Ding! Ding!" went Trolley, and off they went.
As they rode, Daniel and Mom sang together.

"We're going to the post office, I wonder what we'll get?
Won't you ride along with me? Ride along!
Won't you ride along with me?"

89

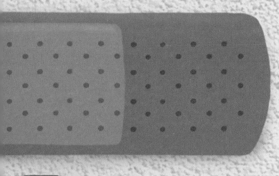

As Trolley rolled along Main Street, Daniel saw Prince Wednesday and his mom. "Can we go say hi?" asked Daniel.

"Absolutely," answered Mom.

"Ding! Ding!" went Trolley as Daniel and Mom Tiger stopped in front of Dr. Anna's office.

But when Daniel saw Prince Wednesday . . . he looked different!

"Prince Wednesday? You look different," said Daniel. "You're not wearing your glasses."

"You look different too!" said Prince Wednesday. "You're not wearing your red sweater."

"My red sweater was dirty. My mom put it in the wash," said Daniel. "Where are your glasses?"

"I was spinning around and around, and my glasses fell onto the ground," said Prince Wednesday. "Dr. Anna is fixing them."

 "You can change your hair, or what you wear, but no matter what you do, you're still you!"

Daniel and Prince Wednesday decided to do something that only they knew how to do . . . their supersecret song and dance. "Shoo be shoo be shooooooo," they sang.

"You're still the same dancing Prince Wednesday!" said Daniel. Prince Wednesday giggled. "You're still the same singing Daniel! Shoo be shoo!"

Just then Dr. Anna came out of her office, holding Prince Wednesday's glasses.

"Here are your glasses, Prince Wednesday," said Dr. Anna. "They're all fixed."

"Thank you, Dr. Anna," said Prince Wednesday as he put his glasses back on. "I can see everything clearly again!"

"It's time for us to go to the post office," said Mom Tiger.

"Okay, bye!" said Daniel, and he and his mom walked along the street to the post office.

At the post office, Daniel was handed a package.

Daniel opened the package and found a new red sweater! "Would you like to put it on?" asked Mom.

Daniel thought about it and then shook his head. "No, thanks. I kind of like my blue sweater, and I want to keep wearing it today."

And Daniel wore his blue sweater for the rest of the day.

Did you ever have to wear something new? What was it? I looked a little different in my blue sweater today, but I learned that I was still me on the inside. Ugga Mugga!

99

Daniel Chooses to Be Kind

It was a beautiful day in the neighborhood when Trolley drove up with King Friday. "I wonder what kings do all day?" Daniel said. "Maybe King Friday can tell us!"

"King Friday! King Friday! I have a question. What is it like being king?" asked Daniel.

"Hmmm...," said King Friday. "If you really want to know ... then I hereby declare you King Daniel for the day!"

"Really? Thank you!" said Daniel.

"King Daniel, you'll need to do everything left on this royal list," said King Friday. "First, go to the bakery and pick up the most royally delicious treat. Next, go to the music shop and get the loudest instrument. And last, come to the castle with those two things."

"Grr-ific! Lets go!" said Daniel.

"Wait!" said King Friday. "I haven't told you the most important thing about being a king. You must be kind."

"What's kind?" asked Daniel.

"Being kind is doing a nice thing for someone, like helping them or giving them a hug. You can choose to be kind," explained King Friday.

"Okay!" answered Daniel. "I will be king and be kind. Let's go to the bakery!"

At the bakery Daniel and Mom saw that Baker Aker was very busy finishing his itsy-bitsy rolls.

Daniel remembered King Friday's words, "You can choose to be kind." He announced, "I can help you, Baker Aker!" and began working on the rolls.

"Thank you, Daniel," said Baker Aker.

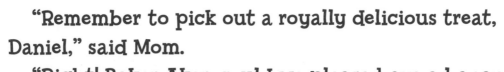

"Remember to pick out a royally delicious treat, Daniel," said Mom.

"Right! Baker Aker, could we please have a banana muffin to bring to the castle?" asked Daniel. "It's my royal duty as king for the day."

"Good choice," said Baker Aker.

"Thanks! Have a royally grr-ific day!" said Daniel as they left the bakery.

Daniel and Mom were on their way when they saw O the Owl and his Uncle X.

"Royal greetings!" said Daniel.

"Hi, Daniel! I like your crown," said O. And just then his treat fell on the ground. "Oh no!" cried O. "That was my special treat!"

"O looks so sad. Maybe a new treat would help," said Daniel. "I think it would be kind to give O the banana muffin, don't you?"

"O, would you want this treat? It's a banana muffin," said Daniel.

"Really? You want to give it to me?" asked O. "Oh, thank you, thank you, thank you, Daniel. That is so kind of you!"

"You're welcome," said Daniel. "Being kind is tigertastic! I have to go to the music store now. Bye, O!"
"Good-bye, King Daniel!" O said.

Daniel and Mom went to the music shop. "Hi, Music Man Stan!" Daniel said.

"Well, hi there, Daniel," said Music Man Stan. Suddenly a gust of wind blew away all his papers. "Oh no!" he exclaimed.

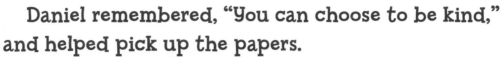

Daniel remembered, "You can choose to be kind," and helped pick up the papers.

"Thanks a bunch, Daniel," said Music Man Stan. They went inside the music shop.

"Now, how can I help you?" asked Music Man Stan.

"I'm king for the day, and I am here to pick out the loudest instrument to take to the castle!" said Daniel.

"Well, pick out any one you would like," said Music Man Stan.

"I wonder which instrument makes the loudest sound," said Daniel.

He tried the triangle. *Ding!* It was not very loud.

He tried the maracas. *Shh, shh, shh, shake, shake, shake.* They were not very loud either.

And next, he tried the cymbals. *CRASH!* That was really loud! "I choose the cymbals," said Daniel.

"Now all I have to do is go to the castle. I don't have a royally delicious treat," said Daniel. "But at least I have a loud instrument for King Friday. Thank you, Music Man Stan!"

"You're welcome, King Daniel," said Music Man Stan.

On their way to the castle, Daniel and Mom Tiger saw Miss Elaina and Lady Elaine playing. Just then Miss Elaina dropped her doll in the mud. Miss Elaina began to cry.

"Oh no," said Daniel. "Miss Elaina is sad. I want to help her."

Daniel walked up to Miss Elaina. "I'm sorry you're sad, Miss Elaina," said Daniel. "Would this cheer you up?" Daniel played the cymbals, *CRASH!*

Miss Elaina smiled. "I love, love, love the cymbals! They are so loud! Can I have a turn?" she asked.

Miss Elaina banged the cymbals together. "This is the best!" she said.

Miss Elaina was so happy! Daniel wanted to give her the cymbals, but he was supposed to take them to the castle. Then Daniel remembered, "You can choose to be kind!"

"Miss Elaina, I declare that you can keep the cymbals," said Daniel.

"Oh, thank you, thank you!" she said as she played happily.

"That was very kind, King Daniel," said Mom. "Now we better finish your royal duties."

"Okay," said Daniel. "Hear ye! Hear ye! King Daniel has to go to the castle now. Good-bye!"

As they arrived at the castle, King Friday announced, "Welcome, King Daniel! Did you bring everything I asked for?"

"No, King Friday," Daniel answered. "I don't have anything. I guess I didn't do a good job as king."

"Actually, Daniel," said King Friday, "being king is about helping others and being kind. I heard that you have found lots of ways to be kind today. I hereby declare that you have done your job as king very well!"

"Thank you, King Friday!" said Daniel.

"It was fun being king today. Did you know there are so many ways to be kind? Even the little ways make people so happy!" said Daniel. "Remember to be kind! Ugga Mugga!"

Daniel Plays in the Snow

It was time to get dressed, so Daniel went to his bedroom.
"Think about what you're going to do, and pick the clothes that are right for you," said Dad.
"I know just what to wear," said Daniel.

"I'll wear my swimsuit!" He giggled.
"No!" Dad laughed. "It's too cold to swim today!"

"Okay, I'll wear my raincoat!" Daniel smiled.
"No." Dad chuckled. "It's not raining today. It's snowing."

"Then I'll wear my cozy red sweater," said Daniel.
"Good thinking," said Dad. "That sweater will keep you warm and toasty."

Daniel looked out the window. "Look at all the snowflakes," he said. "It looks like snow people should be living out there!"

Daniel imagined that a family of snow tigers lived in his yard.

Ding-dong! Miss Elaina was at the door.

"Hiya, toots! It's snowing! It's snowing!" exclaimed Miss Elaina.

"Hi, Miss Elaina," said Daniel. "Do you want to play outside?"

"Yes!" said Miss Elaina. "And I brought our space helmets, so we can be astronauts and zoom to the moon!"

"Tigertastic!" said Daniel. "Let's go!"

"Just a minute," said Mom Tiger. "Think about what you're going to do, and choose the clothes that are right for you."

"It's cold outside," said Daniel. "So I need to wear something warm."

Daniel decided to wear his snowsuit and his boots.

"One boot, two boots," he said as he put them on his feet.

But Daniel did not want to put on his hat and mittens.

"I can't be an astronaut with a hat and mittens! I want to wear my space helmet!" said Daniel.

Mom Tiger said, "Your paws are going to get very cold."

"It's no fun to be cold, toots," said Miss Elaina. "I think I'll wear my hat."

"I won't be cold!" said Daniel.

"All right, Daniel," said Mom Tiger. "You can try it, but come back in if you get cold."

Daniel and Miss Elaina played out in the snow.

"Help me roll a snowball!" said Miss Elaina. But Daniel didn't move.

Miss Elaina tried again. "Help me make a snow astronaut!" she exclaimed. But Daniel still didn't move!

"Why aren't you playing?" asked Miss Elaina.

"I'm coooooold!" Daniel exclaimed. He ran back to the house.

When Mom opened the door, Daniel hurried inside. "Think about what you're going to do, and pick the clothes that are right for you," he said. "I am going to play in the snow, so I need my hat and mittens. The snow is cold!" He pulled on his hat and mittens.

I love playing in the snow, but it sure is cold! If you ever play in the snow, remember to wear your hat and mittens. Ugga Mugga!

Calm at the Restaurant

It was a beautiful night in the neighborhood, and the Tiger family was doing something special for dinner.

"We're going to meet our friend Jodi Platypus at the neighborhood restaurant!" Daniel said.

Daniel was so excited, he could barely sit still! Daniel sang and danced around the yard as they waited for Trolley.

"Restaurant, restaurant, res-tau-rant!" he cheered. He was feeling silly.

When Trolley arrived, Daniel climbed aboard and even danced on his seat! He kept cheering, "Restaurant, restaurant, res-tau-rant!"

"I know you're excited," said Dad Tiger, "but there are times to be silly and times to be calm. Right now we need to be calm so we can ride safely on Trolley." Dad helped Daniel calm down by singing,

 "Give a squeeze, nice and slow,
take a deep breath and let it go."

Daniel squeezed his sillies out, and when he felt calm, he buckled his seat belt, and Trolley was able to start moving.

When Trolley pulled up on Main Street, the Tiger family hopped off and walked toward the restaurant.

"Since we're not on Trolley anymore, can we be silly now?" Daniel wondered.

Mom and Dad thought that was a grr-ific idea. They all sang and danced their way down the sidewalk!

But when they arrived at the quiet restaurant, Daniel knew it was time to be calm again. He sang,

 "Give a squeeze, nice and slow,
take a deep breath and let it go."

Then he took a great big breath in and out. That made him feel more calm.

Jodi and her mom were already at the restaurant when Daniel's family arrived. Prince Tuesday showed the Tigers over to their table and handed everyone a menu. "I hope you are all royally excited, because tonight is . . . taco night!" Prince Tuesday said.

"Tigertastic!" said Daniel.

"Yippy Skippy!" said Jodi.

They were both so excited for taco night.

"I'm going to make the biggest taco ever," said Jodi.

She sang loudly and wiggled in her chair.

 "Crunchy shell and juicy tomatoes!"

Daniel joined in on the fun, singing,

 "Stringy cheese and lots of lettuce!"

Daniel and Jodi bounced in their seats excitedly. "Whoa!" said Prince Tuesday, who was right behind them and carrying a tray of food. "Careful there, kiddos."

Daniel was being so silly, he accidentally knocked into Prince Tuesday's tray.

"Daniel," said Mom Tiger, "we are in a restaurant, and that means it's time to be calm."

"You too, Jodi," said Dr. Plat.

Daniel showed Jodi how to calm down while they waited for their food. They sang,

*"Give a squeeze, nice and slow,
take a deep breath and let it go."*

Daniel and Jodi both felt calm. "But it's still very hard to wait," said Jodi.

"Maybe we can pretend while we wait," said Daniel. He imagined that there were tacos . . . everywhere!

A taco for you, a taco for me!
My taco world is the place to be.
I love tacos with shredded lettuce and stringy cheese!
From my wonderful taco world!
I'll build my taco way up high
Built with toppings from the sky!
I love tacos with sour cream and juicy tomatoes!
From my wonderful taco world.
My taco world is the place to be.
Tacos for you and me!

Imagining made the waiting go by quickly. Prince Tuesday returned with lots of yummy taco shells and toppings.

"Now we can put whatever we want in our tacos," said Daniel.

Jodi put lots of cheese and beans in her taco. Daniel added lots of crunchy lettuce and tomatoes.

The tacos were delicious! Daniel and Jodi sang,

"Tacos for you and tacos for me!"

But this time they sang very softly and very calmly. "I like being silly, but it feels good to be calm, too," Daniel whispered. "Ugga Mugga."

Munch your Lunch!

It was a beautiful day in the neighborhood, and Daniel's dad was dropping him off at school.

"Guess what, Dad?" said Daniel. "Today we're getting our classroom jobs."

"That's exciting," said Dad Tiger. "I wonder what your job will be."

"I want to be the line leader," said Daniel. "I've even been practicing! Watch!" Daniel giggled as he marched into school. "Follow me!"

Inside the classroom, Dad Tiger gave Daniel his lunch box.

"Here's your lunch, Daniel," said Dad Tiger. "I put a surprise in it for later."

"You did?" said Daniel. "What is it?"

"You have to wait until lunch to find out!" Dad Tiger chuckled. "Now it's time for you to play. I'll see you after school!"

"Okay," said Daniel. "Bye, Dad!"

Miss Elaina walked over to Daniel Tiger . . . backward. "Daniel, guess what classroom job I want to have?"

"I don't know!" said Daniel.

"Backward helper!" Miss Elaina giggled. "Except that's not really a job."

"I want to be line leader," said Daniel.

It was circle time, and Teacher Harriet began to tell everyone what their classroom jobs were going to be.

Lights helper was . . . Katerina Kittycat!

Plant helper was . . . O the Owl! "Hoo hoo, yay!"

Snowball the bunny's helper was . . . Prince Wednesday!

And line leader was . . . Miss Elaina!

"Miss Elaina is line leader?" asked Daniel. "But . . . what's my job?"

"Daniel, your job is lunch helper," said Teacher Harriet. "You will pass out all of the lunch boxes at lunchtime."

"I don't want to be lunch helper," Daniel said sadly. "I want to be line leader."

Circle time was over, and everyone got up to do their jobs. Everyone was excited . . . except for Daniel.

It was lunchtime, and everyone was hungry.

"It's time to munch your lunch," Teacher Harriet said.

"I'm rrroyally hungry!" said Prince Wednesday.

"Me too! Hoo hoo," said O the Owl. "But where are our lunches?"

Daniel remembered that he was the lunch helper. Nobody could eat their lunch because he didn't do his job! "Being lunch helper is an important job!" said Daniel. "Without me, there's no lunch!"

Daniel gave his friends their lunch boxes.
Daniel gave the book lunch box to O the Owl and
the Museum-Go-Round lunch box to Miss Elaina.

158

Daniel gave the royal crown lunch box to Prince Wednesday and the ballet lunch box with the pink ribbon on it to Katerina Kittycat.

At last, Daniel sat down with his tiger lunch box. "I wonder what I have for lunch today?" he said.

Daniel opened up his lunch. On top of the food he found a note! It was from Dad Tiger and said:

No matter what your classroom job is, you are special to me! Ugga Mugga! Love, Dad Tiger

Dad Tiger's note made Daniel so happy, and his lunch was deeelicious!

Daniel loved his dad's lunch box note, and he loved being lunch helper, too!

"What do you like to eat for lunch?" asks Daniel. "Ugga Mugga!"

No matter what your classroom job is, you are special to me! Ugga Mugga! Love, Dad Tiger

Big Enough to Help

In the backyard, Dad Tiger was building Daniel a playhouse.

"It looks just like our house!" said Daniel, giggling. "Except it doesn't have a door."

"I'm going to put the door on with my hammer," said Dad.

"Can I use the hammer?" asked Daniel.

"I'm sorry, Daniel," replied Dad. "A hammer is a grown-up tool."

"I'm not big enough to help build my playhouse," said Daniel sadly.

"Everyone is big enough to do something," said Dad. "And you are big enough to be my helper tiger and hold the door in place while I hammer."

"I can do that!" said Daniel.
Bang, bang, bang went the hammer as Daniel helped Dad.

165

"Now it's time to paint the door," said Dad.

"Am I big enough to help?" asked Daniel.

"Yes!" said Dad. "Can you help me pick the paint colors?"

"I can do that!" said Daniel as he picked red, blue, and yellow paint.

"I'll paint the top of the door, and you paint the bottom," said Dad. "Deal?"

"Deal," answered Daniel.

Swish, swish, swish went the paintbrushes as Daniel helped Dad.

Daniel loved painting. He imagined he could paint with his hands . . .

. . . and his feet.

"Time to put on the doorbell," said Dad. "I have to use my screwdriver."

"Can I use the screwdriver?" asked Daniel.

"I'm sorry, Daniel," said Dad. "A screwdriver is a grown-up tool."

"Does that mean I can't be your helper tiger anymore?" asked Daniel.

"Everyone is big enough to do something," explained Dad. "Can you help hand me my tools?"
"Sure!" said Daniel.

First, Dad asked for a pencil.

"Pencil!" said Daniel as he handed it to Dad.

Then Dad asked for glue. "No glue!" said Daniel.

"Uh-oh," said Dad. "We need the glue to put the doorbell on the playhouse."

"I'll find it!" said Daniel. "I'm big enough to do that!"

Daniel looked in the kitchen for the glue, and he found his mom. She was using the glue!

"Will you help me?" asked Mom Tiger. "I need to glue a handle on this cabinet."

"Okay," said Daniel.

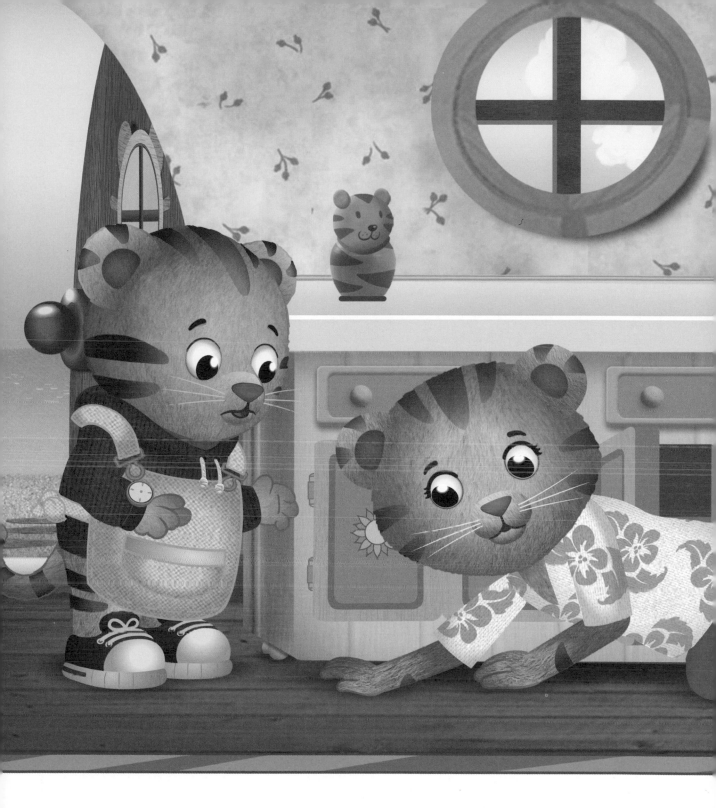

"Whoops!" said Mom. "I dropped the handle! Where did it go?"
Daniel watched as the handle rolled and rolled and rolled until
it stopped right under the cabinet.

"Oh no!" said Mom. "My hand is too big to reach it!"

"I'll get it!" said Daniel. "My hand is just the right size."
Daniel reached and reached and reached until . . .

"Got it!" cried Daniel.
"Thank you, my helper tiger," said Mom.

Daniel finished helping Mom and then brought out the glue to Dad.

"A little glue here, a twist of the screwdriver, and . . . all finished!" said Dad. "Thank you for helping me, my big helper tiger. And now, I think you are big enough to play in your new playhouse."

"I can do that!" said Daniel. He smiled proudly as he stepped inside.

"I like being big enough to play inside my playhouse," said Daniel Tiger. "Everyone is big enough to do something. What are *YOU* big enough to do? Ugga Mugga!"

Daniel Tiger's Day and Night

It's time to get ready for a grr-ific day!
What does Daniel need to do before it's time to play?

"Clothes on, eat breakfast, brush teeth, put on shoes, and off to school."

First, he changes out of his pj's and into his clothes. The red sweater is his favorite, everyone knows.

Now that Daniel is dressed, what's next on the checklist? Let's go to the kitchen and see what's for breakfast.

183

Next, he brushes his teeth until the timer dings.
"Brusha, brusha, brush," Daniel Tiger sings.

DING!

Last, Daniel puts on his shoes before going outside.
Trolley is here! Time to go for a ride.

Some days Daniel goes to the park for a picnic on the grass.

Some days he helps his dad at the store or goes to music class.

Some days he goes to school to learn and play. What is it that YOU are doing today?

When the sun goes down and the moon shines bright, Daniel Tiger gets ready for night. "That was a yummy dinner," Daniel said.

 "Now it's bathtime, pj's, brush teeth, story and song, and off to bed."

Daniel loves bathtime. He gets into the tub.
He splashes in the bubbles. Scrub-a-dub-dub.

After the bath, what do we wear?
Pajamas, of course! Can you find his favorite pair?

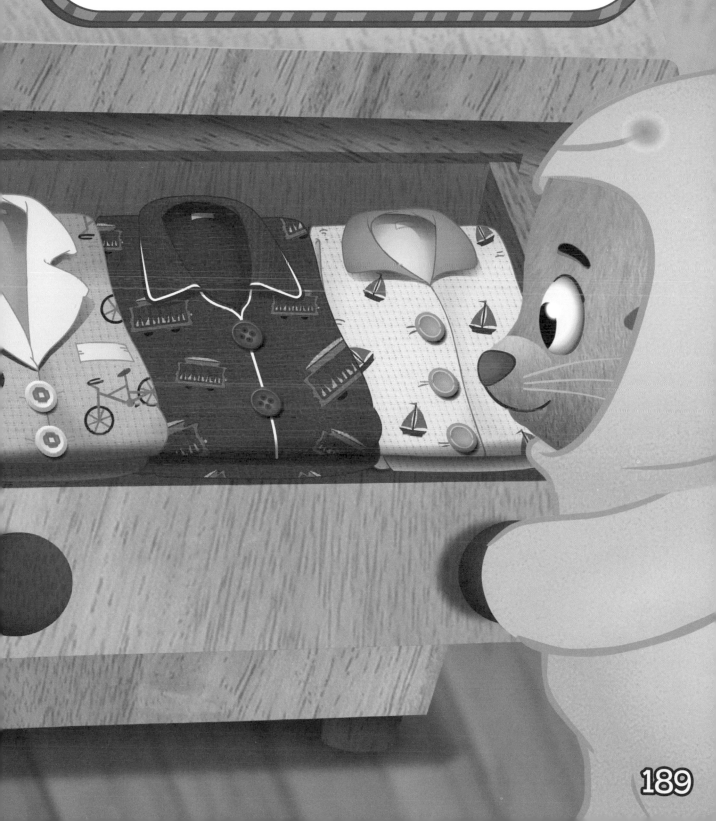

To keep his teeth healthy and bright,
Daniel brushes both day and night.

190

Daniel gets comfy and cozy in bed.
He reads a story, sings a song, and rests his tired head.

*"It's time to sleep. The day is done.
Let's count down to calm down. 5, 4, 3, 2, 1."*

Daniel holds Tigey and hugs him tight.
It is time to say goodnight.
Ugga Mugga!